# Dear Parents:

Congratulations! Your child is taking the first steps on an exciting journey. The destination? Independent reading!

**STEP INTO READING®** will help your child get there. The program offers five steps to reading success. Each step includes fun stories and colorful art or photographs. In addition to original fiction and books with favorite characters, there are Step into Reading Non-Fiction Readers, Phonics Readers and Boxed Sets, Sticker Readers, and Comic Readers—a complete literacy program with something to interest every child.

## Learning to Read, Step by Step!

### Ready to Read   Preschool–Kindergarten
• big type and easy words • rhyme and rhythm • picture clues
For children who know the alphabet and are eager to begin reading.

### Reading with Help   Preschool–Grade 1
• basic vocabulary • short sentences • simple stories
For children who recognize familiar words and sound out new words with help.

### Reading on Your Own   Grades 1–3
• engaging characters • easy-to-follow plots • popular topics
For children who are ready to read on their own.

### Reading Paragraphs   Grades 2–3
• challenging vocabulary • short paragraphs • exciting stories
For newly independent readers who read simple sentences with confidence.

### Ready for Chapters   Grades 2–4
• chapters • longer paragraphs • full-color art
For children who want to take the plunge into chapter books but still like colorful pictures.

**STEP INTO READING®** is designed to give every child a successful reading experience. The grade levels are only guides; children will progress through the steps at their own speed, developing confidence in their reading.

Remember, a lifetime love of reading starts with a single step!

Step into Reading, Random House, and the Random House colophon are registered trademarks of Penguin Random House LLC.

Visit us on the Web!
StepIntoReading.com
rhcbooks.com

Educators and librarians, for a variety of teaching tools, visit us at RHTeachersLibrarians.com

ISBN 978-0-525-64827-7 (trade) — ISBN 978-0-525-64828-4 (lib. bdg.)

Printed in the United States of America   10 9 8 7 6 5 4 3 2 1

STEP INTO READING®

2
STEP
READING WITH HELP

nickelodeon

# Nazboo's Kazoo!

by Delphine Finnegan
illustrated by Dave Aikins

Random House 🏠 New York

Shimmer, Shine, and Leah
go to the market.
They meet Gita.

She is the Music Genie!

Gita has a surprise.

It is a magic kazoo!
The kazoo makes
magic extra powerful
whenever it is played.

The first wish of the day!
Leah wishes for
a balloon for Shimmer.
Gita plays
the magic kazoo.

The balloon grows
really big!
Shimmer floats up high.
She lets go of the balloon.
She floats down.

Zeta and Nazboo shop
at the market.
The genies bump
into Zeta.

Zeta drops her bags.
The genies drop
their kazoo case.
The kazoo falls out.

Shine picks up

Zeta's bottles and the case.

She does not see

the kazoo!

The genies fly away.

Nazboo finds the kazoo.

He thinks it is a toy.

He keeps it!

Zeta makes a potion
back at her lair.
She says a spell.

Nazboo plays the kazoo.
The magic potion
grows stronger
from the kazoo music!

Zeta thinks it is
from her magic.
Nazboo's kazoo music
annoys her.

The genies learn that
the kazoo is missing!
The genies turn back.

Zeta goes back, too.
Her potion draws
all the gems from the market
as Nazboo plays.

The genies chase
Zeta through the market.
Zeta's potions
slow them down,
but only when Nazboo
plays the kazoo.

Zeta does not like
the sound of the kazoo.
She makes Nazboo
stop playing.

The genies have a plan.
Shimmer grants Leah's
second wish of the day.
The kazoo gets
louder!

Zeta throws away
the loud kazoo.
The genies catch it.

Zeta's potions
are not as strong
as they were.
Now she understands
all the kazoo can do!

The genies return the gems.
Leah has a third wish—
and Nazboo gets a new toy!